THE DRAGON KITE

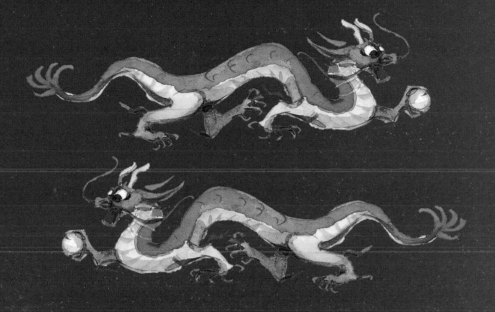

Kenneth Steven

illustrated
by Karin Littlewood

Long ago in a village in China, a boy called Chang lived with his father. The village sat in a valley near a huge volcano that sometimes roared and spat and shook the ground.

Many of the boys in the village played rough and noisy games. But Chang sat quietly with his father, making kites to sell in the town.

They worked in a tiny room at the back of their house. Chang's father cut and sewed the kites with threads of silk and Chang painted them.

The people in the town loved their kites, but the ones they loved most were the dragons. Some dragon kites were huge and some were fierce. Some had big, bulging eyes and some had long bodies and scaly tails that twisted and twirled and sang in the wind.

During the long summer evenings, everyone gathered around the largest tree in the centre of the village, to listen to the old storyteller. Sometimes, his stories were scary, and his scariest ones were about ferocious dragons that roamed the world and were always hungry.

Chang longed to see one. "Where can I find a dragon, Father?" he asked.

"There are no dragons left in the world, my son," replied his father. "There are only stories of dragons. But I will make you the largest and most beautiful dragon kite in the world."

Chang waited and waited, while his father worked on the dragon kite.

"When will my kite be ready, Father?" asked Chang.

"When the wild winds blow in the springtime, your kite will be ready, my son."

One warm spring evening, Chang's kite was ready. "It is beautiful. Thank you, Father," said Chang and went happily off to bed.

Very early next morning, a loud rattling noise shook Chang's window. He was terrified. But it was only the sound of the wind racing past his window and rushing through the trees outside.

"I will try out my new kite!" he whispered to himself.

He tiptoed through the house, along the path and into the fields. The wind grew wilder. It howled through the trees, whipped the leaves from their branches and battered the windows of the sleeping village.

"Fly, dragon kite, fly. Up to the sky!" shouted Chang and threw his kite into the air. The kite whirled and whirled above his head.

Suddenly, a blast of wind, stronger than all the rest, tore Chang's beautiful kite right out of his hands. His terrible scream was swept away with the wind. He stood stock still and stared, and then he ran.

He ran faster than he had ever done before. He jumped into the air and stretched his arms, but he landed back on the ground and the kite rose higher and higher, driven by the mighty wind.

Chang watched in horror as his kite grew smaller and smaller. He watched it rise until it looked like a bird. It flew towards the mountains and he watched it shrink until it was no bigger than an insect. It swirled around the open mouth of the volcano and disappeared.

That night, Chang tossed and turned and could not sleep. As he lay awake in the early morning, he made a plan. "I will climb that volcano and bring my kite home."

He dressed quietly and stepped into the yard. In the distance, the sun, like an enormous ripe orange, rose over the village. The birds sang and the flowers dripped with early morning dew.

Chang ran through the village, into the forest and headed for the high mountains.

The path grew steeper and steeper. He scrambled over pebbles and ran between great boulders, following a trail of bright kite threads strewn across the side of the volcano.

He struggled with clinging vines and sharp broken branches, but he ran on, growing more and more tired.

At last he stopped. The earth shook beneath his feet and strange howling noises surrounded him. Then he spied two long kite threads trailing into the gaping mouth of the volcano.

Chang crept down and down into a deep, dark echoing cavern. Slimy, slithering shapes slapped his face and curled around his legs. He cried out and his voice echoed around the enormous space. He wanted to turn back, but he had lost the way.

Chang wrapped his arms around his chest to stop the loud thumping of his heart. He crouched down. "I must escape," he groaned.

Near his feet, he spied another trail of golden threads. As he reached out to touch one, a terrible cry swept through the cave and loud sobs echoed all around him.

When Chang opened his eyes again, he spied a sliver of light in the grim darkness. He waited and then crept towards it. "That must be the way out. It has to be... I will have to leave my kite behind," he muttered miserably, and headed towards the light.

Suddenly, the ground gave way beneath his feet and he tumbled, head over heels into a gigantic cave.

The brightness dazzled him and then he saw it. A dragon sat in the centre of a huge cavern, on top of a mountain of glistening jewels. His heavy eyelids covered his bulging eyes. His mouth was half open and his huge body shook.

Terrified, Chang stood still and watched him. Lying at the feet of the enormous creature was his kite. "If I can grab it and run… ever so quietly…" Chang whispered to himself.

He edged closer and closer. Just as he reached out, the dragon opened one huge eye and glared at him.

Chang froze. He was sure he was going to die. He crouched into a ball and hid his face in his hands. "Father!" he groaned. "I will never see you again," and he waited to be eaten alive.

Chang waited, but nothing happened.

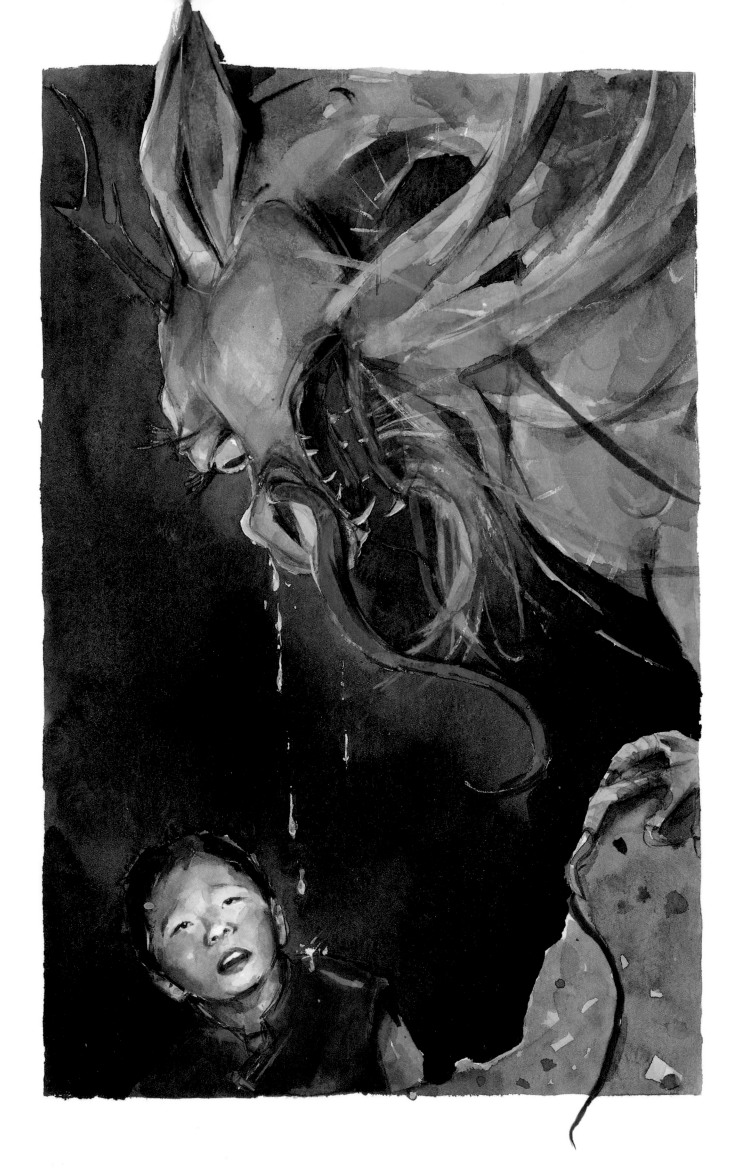

Then suddenly, a sniff and a horrible sob escaped from the dragon. Two huge teardrops rolled down his cheeks. The dragon was crying! But why?

"I don't want to hurt you! Everyone is afraid of me. Everyone hates me. I'm so lonely!" sobbed the enormous creature. "What's your name?"

Chang's mouth fell open, but he could not speak.

"Who are you? I won't eat you," begged the dragon. "Will you be my friend?"

Chang leaped to his feet. He darted across the cave. In his terror, he had forgotten his kite.

"No. Don't go. Is this yours?" roared the dragon.

Chang stopped and looked at the dragon again. The huge creature was really very sad. "My name is Chang. The kite is mine. Thank you."

"Listen, please listen, Chang. Let me explain," begged the dragon. "I have been alone for more than a hundred years… Then yesterday I saw this beautiful creature swaying and swirling in the skies high above my lonely home. I flew out to greet her and we danced together in the wind. I had found a friend, or so I thought. I believed that, after all, I was not the only dragon in the whole world.

"But once we came in here, out of the wind, I found that all I had was a kite. Here she has lain ever since, with an angry face and staring eyes. I'm more lonely than ever! Please be my friend!" begged the dragon.

"Yes, I will," said Chang. "But I have to go home now. I must not be late. Thanks again. Good bye!"

"Where do you live, Chang?" the dragon wailed. "Will you take me with you? It's so lonely here! I won't hurt anyone.

"Long, long ago, when all the dragons in the world were killed, I escaped and hid in this volcano. I have lived here alone for more than a hundred years."

Chang looked into the sad eyes of the dragon and felt sorry for him. "I **will** be your friend. I will take you home with me."

"Thank you! Thank you, Chang!" roared the dragon. "Come. Climb onto my back and I will take you out of this place. Then, you must show me the way to your village."

The dragon's huge body swept upwards at great speed, until they soared towards the sky. Out in the fresh cool air, Chang breathed deeply and looked around.

"There! That's the way to my village."

They flew, down and down, lower and lower. Chang's father and all the villagers gathered in the village square, terrified to see Chang, perched on the back of the enormous beast.

"Don't be afraid!" Chang called out. "This is the one and only dragon left in the world and he is lonely."

The villagers ran into their homes and there they stayed.

"Father, this dragon won't hurt anyone! He wants to be our friend. Can you help?" asked Chang.

Chang's father sat thinking for a very long time. He then made a secret plan.

When it was time for the New Year celebrations to begin, Chang's father appeared in the village square. He carried a dragon made of the most beautiful silks.

The village people came out of their houses and scrambled under the silken dragon. Then they set off for a parade through the village. Chang, his dragon and his kite flew high above them.

After that day, the villagers lost their fear of the dragon. They helped to build him a home near the village where he lived happily ever after.

Dragons in China

There are many legends in China about the different kinds of dragons, each with their own characteristics and powers. The dragon in this story is a winged dragon, one of the oldest and most powerful.

The dragon is one of the symbols of the Chinese zodiac and these creatures play an important part in many Chinese festivals.

Chinese New Year around the world

Many people of Chinese heritage have made their homes all over the world. Today, London, Melbourne, Toronto, New York, Los Angeles and San Francisco are some of the cities where Chinese New Year is celebrated in style.

In China, New Year is celebrated between late January and mid-February. Great preparation is made for this event. Some people clean their homes thoroughly, pay off any debts, buy new clothes and have their hair cut. On New Year's Eve, families gather for a grand meal. Amazing displays of fireworks light up the sky to send off the old year and to welcome the new one. On New Year's Day, beautiful lions and dragons, made from dazzling fabrics, dance through the streets.

Kung Hei Fat Choy!*

* Happy New Year!

Kites

Kites were invented in China, more than 2,000 years ago. There are different stories about how people got the idea for making them. One story is that someone's hat blew off and flew in the wind, still attached to its wearer by the neckband. Another story is that a war leader wanted a way to show off his banner and fly it high above his troops.

In olden times, kites were used in war. One story goes that a general flew kites carrying harps over his enemy's army at night. The enemy was scared by the noise and fled in terror. Chinese Emperors also used kites to send signals to their troops.

Some people believed that by flying kites they would avoid bad luck. A kite could ward off evil spirits and the higher it flew the richer a person would become. Kite-flying was considered a healthy pastime.

When the Chinese invented paper, it became possible for anyone to build a kite. People began to build them in the shape of creatures of folk tales and mythology, including dragons.

For Sylvia with thanks for all the dragons
K.S.

For my Robin
K.L.

THE DRAGON KITE
TAMARIND BOOKS 978 1 870 51684 6

Published in Great Britain by Tamarind Books,
a division of Random House Children's Books
A Random House Group Company

This edition published 2009

3 5 7 9 10 8 6 4 2

Set in Garamond

TAMARIND BOOKS
61-63 Uxbridge Road, London, W5 5SA

www.tamarindbooks.co.uk
www.kidsatrandomhouse.co.uk
www.rbooks.co.uk

Addresses for companies within The Random House group Limited can be
found at: www.randomhouse.co.uk/offices.htm

THE RANDOM HOUSE GROUP Limited Reg. No. 954009

A CIP catalogue record for this book is available from the British Library

Printed and bound in Singapore

OTHER TAMARIND TITLES

TAMARIND READERS:

Reading between the Lions
Ferris Fleet, the Wheelchair Wizard
The Day Ravi Smiled
Hurricane

The Life of Stephen Lawrence
The History of the Steel Band

BIOGRAPHIES:

Barack Obama
Rudolph Walker
Benjamin Zephaniah
Malorie Blackman
Samantha Tross
Baroness Scotland of Asthal
Jim Brathwaite
Lord Taylor of Warwick
Chinwe Roy

AND FOR YOUNGER READERS...

Amina and the Shell
The Silence Seeker
Princess Katrina and the Hair Charmer
Mum's Late
Marty Monster
The Bush
The Feather
Boots for a Bridesmaid
Starlight

To see the rest of our list, please visit our website

www.tamarindbooks.co.uk